Disney's
A Winnie the Pooh First Reader

Pooh's
Fun Time Treasury

Stories by Isabel Gaines

DISNEY
PRESS

NEW YORK

Contents

DISNEY'S
A Winnie the Pooh First Reader
Pooh's Hero Party

by Isabel Gaines

ILLUSTRATED BY Studio Orlando

Pooh's Hero Party

It was a stormy day

in the Hundred-Acre Wood.

The wind blew very hard.

So hard that it blew

Owl's house down.

Christopher Robbin, Eeyore,

and Rabbit came

to see the damage.

"When a house looks like that,"

said Eeyore, "it is time

to find another one.

Owl, I will find a new house for you."

The stormy day turned into

a stormy night.

The Hundred-Acre Wood flooded.

Christopher Robin worried

about Piglet and Pooh.

He did not know where they were.

He went to the edge of

the water and looked around.

Suddenly, Pooh appeared.

He was floating on a chair.

"Pooh!" cried Christopher Robin.

"I am so glad you are safe!

But where is Piglet?"

Just then something floated out

from under Pooh's chair.

It was a honeypot.

"Here I am," Piglet said

from inside the pot.

"Pooh!" Christopher Robin cried

again. "You saved Piglet!"

"I did?" asked Pooh.

"Yes!" Christopher Robin said.

"You are a hero!"

"I am?" asked Pooh.

"Yes," said Christopher Robin.

"When the storm is over,
I will give you a hero party."

Pooh's hero party had just begun when Eeyore walked up.

"I found a house for Owl," he said.

"Great!" said Owl. "Where is it?"

"Follow me," said Eeyore.

Everyone followed Eeyore.

Much to their surprise,

when they got to Owl's house

it turned out to be . . .

. . . Piglet's house!

"Why are we stopping here?"

asked Christopher Robin.

"This is Owl's new house,"

Eeyore proudly said.

"What do you think of it?"

Christopher Robin said,

"It is a nice house, Eeyore, but . . ."

"It is lovely," Kanga added, "but . . ."

"It is the best house

in the world," Piglet said

with a tear in his eye.

Pooh said quietly to Piglet,

"Tell him it is your house."

"No," Piglet said with a sniff.

"This house belongs to Owl."

"But where will *you* live?" asked Rabbit.

"Well," said Piglet, "I will live . . ."

"With me!" said Pooh.

"You will live with me,

right, Piglet?"

"Oh thank you, Pooh," Piglet said.

TRESPASS

WILL

"Piglet, that was
a great thing to do,"
Christopher Robin said.
"You are a hero!" added Rabbit.

Pooh started to think.

"I am a hero for saving Piglet
in the storm," Pooh said.
"Piglet is a hero for giving
his home to Owl."

"Christopher Robin," Pooh asked,
"can we make a one-hero party
into a two-hero party?"

"Of course we can,"

said Christopher Robin.

And that is just what they did.

Can you match the words with the pictures?

Owl

think

house

party

storm

Fill in the missing letters.

Ee_ore

c_air

h_neypot

Pig_et

_ero

36

A Winnie the Pooh First Reader

Pooh's Best Friend

Isabel Gaines

ILLUSTRATED BY Tim Jones

Pooh's Best Friend

One fine spring day,

Winnie the Pooh

got to thinking about friends.

He had many friends.

But who was his *best* friend?

Could it be Owl?

Eeyore?

Or Rabbit?

Tigger?

Kanga?

Or Roo?

And what about Piglet?

Hmm, Pooh thought.

What is a best friend?

I think I shall ask everyone

in the Hundred-Acre Wood.

Pooh licked some honey
from a honeypot,
then headed outside.

First, Pooh asked Owl.

"Owl, what is a best friend?"

"My Great-Aunt Gabby once said,

'A best friend is someone

you can talk to about anything.'"

said Owl.

Pooh and Owl talked about
some things. They talked
about the weather
and Owl's relatives.
But Pooh and Piglet
talked about everything.
They talked about hunting
heffalumps and finding honey.
They talked about the best places
for a picnic.

Next, Pooh asked Rabbit.

"Rabbit, what is a best friend?"

"If you must know,"

replied Rabbit,

"a best friend is someone

who is unselfish."

Pooh liked Rabbit.

But was Rabbit as unselfish as Piglet?

Pooh remembered

all the unselfish things

that Piglet had done for him.

He let Pooh sit by the fire

in his favorite chair.

He gave Pooh the biggest slice

of huckleberry pie.

Next, Pooh asked Eeyore.

"Eeyore, what is a best friend?"

"I wouldn't know, Pooh.

But I suspect it's someone

who remembers your birthday."

Pooh wondered if Eeyore

had ever remembered his birthday.

Once Piglet had thrown

a party for Pooh, complete

with balloons and cake

and honey lemonade.

Next, Pooh asked Tigger.

"Tigger, what is a best friend?"

"Hoo-hoo-*hoo*! That's easy,"
Tigger said.

"A best friend is someone
who sticks around,
even if you bounce him
accidentally."

Hmm, Pooh thought.

I stick around Tigger

when he bounces me.

Then Pooh remembered all the times
that Piglet had stuck around.
Like the time Pooh
had forgotten
to meet Piglet
at the bridge.
And the time
that Pooh had eaten
Piglet's lunch by mistake.

Next, Pooh asked Kanga.

"Kanga, what is a best friend?"

"A best friend, Pooh dear,

is someone who is patient

and kind," said Kanga.

Pooh thought,

that sounds like Kanga.

But then Pooh thought

a little longer.

Kanga had also described Piglet.

Piglet was all of those things

and more.

Piglet was easy to talk to.

He was unselfish and loyal.

And he always remembered

Pooh's birthday.

As Pooh turned to go,

Roo squeaked,

"I know what a best friend is!

A best friend is someone

who asks you to play!"

"You're right, Roo," said Pooh.

"Thank you!"

At that moment, Pooh knew

who his best friend was—Piglet.

Pooh walked along the path

and thought of all the marvelous

things that he and Piglet

had done together.

He saw a daisy and picked it.

He hurried to Piglet's house
and thumped on the door.
"Hello, Piglet!" said Pooh.
"I brought you a daisy."
"How kind of you,"
said Piglet.
"Would you like a piece
of huckleberry pie?"

The two friends sat inside.

But this time, Pooh insisted

that Piglet sit by the fire

in the comfiest chair

and take the biggest piece

of huckleberry pie.

For if Piglet was Pooh's best friend,
Pooh wanted to be his.

A Winnie the Pooh First Reader

Happy Birthday, Eeyore

Adapted by Isabel Gaines

ILLUSTRATED BY Studio Orlando

Happy Birthday,
Eeyore

Eeyore was in his sad spot
when Pooh stopped by.

"Eeyore, why are you
so sad?" Pooh asked.
"It's my birthday," said Eeyore.

"Your birthday?" asked Pooh.

"Of course," said Eeyore.

"Can't you see the presents?"

Pooh looked around.

"No," said Pooh.

"The cake and candles?"
asked Eeyore.

"Well, no," said Pooh.

"Neither can I," Eeyore said sadly.

That gave Pooh an idea.

He said, "Eeyore,

wait right here."

Pooh ran to his house.

Piglet was there

looking for him.

"I must get poor
Eeyore a present,"
Pooh said. "But what?"

Pooh looked

around his house.

He saw a small
honeypot
on his shelf.
"Of course!
Honey!"
cried Pooh.
"Piglet, what are you
giving Eeyore?"
"Well, I could give him
my red balloon,"
Piglet said.

"Good idea," Pooh said.

Piglet went home

to find the balloon.

Pooh left to give

Eeyore his present.

Pooh had not gone far

when he felt strange.

It was as if someone

inside him said,

"Time to eat."

Pooh sat down
and ate the honey
in the honeypot.
He ate and ate.

When he had licked
the last sticky drop,
Pooh asked, "Now,
where was I going?"

"Oh yes—to Eeyore's.
Oh bother! Now what
will I give Eeyore?"
Pooh began to think.

"I know!" said Pooh.

"A honeypot without honey
is a *useful* pot.

Eeyore can put whatever
he wants in it."

At the same time, Piglet carried
a red balloon to Eeyore.
"Hello, Piglet!" he heard
from above.

Piglet looked up.

Owl was flying over him.

Piglet did not see

the tree in his path.

POP! Piglet crashed
into the tree.
"Oh d-d-d-dear," said Piglet.
"The balloon broke."

Piglet arrived
at Eeyore's house.
"Eeyore, here is
a birthday present
for you."

Piglet handed
the broken red balloon
to Eeyore.

Eeyore sadly looked
at the shredded red balloon.
Then Pooh arrived.

"I've brought you

a present, Eeyore," Pooh said.

"It's a useful pot."

Eeyore picked up the balloon
and dropped it in the pot.

"Eeyore, I am glad I gave you
that pot," said Pooh.
"And I am glad
that I gave you something
to put into the pot,"
added Piglet.

Just then, Christopher Robin
and Eeyore's other friends
arrived.

Christopher Robin led them all
to Rabbit's house.

They had a birthday party for Eeyore.

Eeyore did not say much.

But he looked very, very happy.

Disney's
A Winnie the Pooh First Reader
Pooh's Leaf Pile

by Isabel Gaines

ILLUSTRATED BY Francesc Rigol

101

Pooh's Leaf Pile

One lovely fall day,

the air was cool and crisp.

So Pooh and Piglet decided

to play outside.

They stepped out Pooh's door.

As they walked,

Pooh heard a strange

crunching noise.

"Piglet," said Pooh,

"do you hear that noise?"

Pooh and Piglet stopped and listened.

But they didn't hear anything.

"Look!" said Pooh.

"The trees have lost

all their leaves."

They continued on their walk.

Crunch crunch, they heard again.

"Piglet," said Pooh,
"I believe that noise
is the sound of our feet
stepping on the leaves.
See, they've fallen to the ground."

"Oh my!" said Piglet.

"Look at all the colors."

Just then, Rabbit arrived.

"Pooh!" he cried.

"Look at your yard!"

"Isn't it pretty?" said Pooh.

"Your yard is a mess," said Rabbit.

"We must clean it up.

Get the rakes!

We will rake the leaves

into one big pile."

"But they look so pretty," said Pooh.

"They will look pretty in a pile, too," said Rabbit.

Pooh, Piglet, and Rabbit raked and raked and raked.

As they finished,

Tigger and Roo stopped by.

"That's a terrific leaf pile,"

said Tigger. "Perfect for bouncing!"

Tigger and Roo bounced

into the pile of leaves.

Pooh and Piglet jumped

into the pile, too.

"Roo," said Tigger,

"let's tell everyone

about Pooh's leaf pile."

Tigger and Roo bounced off

to get the others.

"Oh no!" Rabbit cried.

"Our neat pile of leaves

is now a big mess!"

"Perhaps we should

do something else

with them," said Piglet.

"Yes," said Rabbit.

"Something that's not so messy.

Let's ask Christopher Robin

what to do."

Everyone gathered around Pooh's leaf pile.

They waited for Rabbit

and Christopher Robin.

When they finally arrived,

Christopher Robin said,

"Let's make crafts with the leaves.

First, we will make a collage."

All the friends gathered

leaves, acorns, pinecones, and nuts.

Christopher Robin helped them

paste everything onto

a big piece of paper.

"Great job!" said Christopher Robin.

Next Christopher Robin
had everyone tape leaves
onto a piece of paper.
Then they painted the paper,
leaves and all.

When they were done painting,

they carefully removed the leaves

from the paper.

"Leaf shapes!" said Piglet.

For the last craft,

everyone placed a leaf

underneath a piece of paper.

Then they peeled the paper wrapping

off a crayon.

They rolled the crayon

over the paper.

"A leaf appeared on my paper!"

said Roo. "It's magic!"

"Crafts are fun," said Tigger.

"But Tiggers like bouncing

in leaves the best."

"So do Roos!" said Roo.

"No!" shouted Rabbit.

"Please don't make another mess!"

"My house is always

full of leaves," said Eeyore.

"It's not so bad."

"So come on, Rabbit," said Tigger.

"Let's get messy!"

Tigger grabbed Rabbit

by the hand and bounced him

into the middle of the pile.

Everyone else jumped in after them.

Rabbit started to giggle.

Then he let out a big laugh.

He liked playing in the leaves!

Rabbit picked up

an armful of leaves

and tossed them into the air.

"Happy fall!" he shouted.

Can you match the words with the pictures?

leaf

Rabbit

rake

pile

Pooh